Y0-BVR-905

Leonardo
DA VINCI

Stewart Ross

RAINTREE
STECK-VAUGHN
RSVP PUBLISHERS

A Harcourt Company

Austin   New York
www.raintreesteckvaughn.com

Copyright Permissions, Steck-Vaughn Company,
P.O. Box 26015, Austin, TX 78755.

Published by Raintree Steck-Vaughn Publishers,
an imprint of Steck-Vaughn Company

Library of Congress Cataloging-in-Publication Data

Ross, Stewart.
    Leonardo da Vinci / Stewart Ross.
      p. cm.—(Scientists who made history)
    Includes bibliographical references and index.
    Summary: A biography of the versatile Renaissance artist in the context of his times, describing some of his achievements in painting, architecture, engineering, sculpture, and science.
    ISBN 0-7398-5223-X
      1. Leonardo da Vinci, 1452–1519—Juvenile literature.
    2. Artists—Italy—Biography—Juvenile literature. 3. Scientists—Italy—Biography—Juvenile literature. 4. Renaissance—Italy—Juvenile literature. [1. Leonardo da Vinci, 1452-1519. 2. Artists. 3. Scientists.] I. Leonardo, da Vinci, 1452-1519. II. Title. III. Series.

N6923.L33 R66 2002
709'.2—dc21
[B]   2001048962

Printed in Italy. Bound in the United States.

1 2 3 4 5 6 7 8 9 LB 07 06 05 04 03 02

Picture Acknowledgments: AKG 4, 10, 11, 13, 15, 16, 17, 18, 20, 27b, 30l, 31, 32, 33, 34t, 35, 36b, 37, 38, 39t, 39b, 40, 41, 43; Bridgeman Art Library 5, 22, 23, 24, 25, 36t; Bridgeman Art Library/Musee Conde 14; Bridgeman Art Library/National Gallery of Scotland 12; Fotomas Index 29b; Hodder Wayland Picture Library 6, 19, 26, 28t, 28b, 42t, 42b; Mary Evans Picture Library *cover, title page,* 7tl, 7b, 9, 21, 29t; Scala 34b; Topham Picturepoint 7tr, 30r.

Contents

From Another World

THE ROYAL PARTY cantered noisily across the narrow wooden bridge over the Amasse River and set off up the slope toward the château of Cloux. Riding at the head of the group, the handsome young king looked worried.

The news was bad. Leonardo, his First Painter, Architect, and Mechanic, his most prized and famous subject, had been ill. Paralyzed, some reports said.

The 24-year-old Francis I rode swiftly up to the castle entrance, swung down from the saddle, and strode past the guards into the entrance hall. Seeing a servant girl, he called her to him and bombarded her with questions about Leonardo.

I Am Left-Handed

Flustered, the girl did her best to answer the king's questions. She directed him to a room on the first floor. Francis bounded up the stone steps, paused for a second before a heavy oak door, then gently pushed it open.

LEFT: *A Renaissance king: Francis I of France (ruled 1515–1547), who greatly admired Leonardo and gave him generous shelter during the last years of the genius' life.*

Before him, at a table covered with papers, sat a dignified-looking old man. From beneath his blue cap strands of wispy white hair fell almost to his shoulders. His full beard was equally long, equally white. In his left hand he held a quill pen. His right hand hung by his side.

The king was clearly delighted to find Leonardo better than he had hoped. A broad smile spread across his face as he walked into the room.

Leonardo turned slowly toward the king and smiled back at him, his bright eyes twinkling. He explained that he was not paralyzed. His right side did not work as well as it had, but as he was left-handed he could write, draw, and paint as well as he had ever done.

IN THEIR OWN WORDS

As Leonardo neared the end of his life, he reflected on how it had been spent;

"As a day well-spent brings happy sleep, so a life well-used brings happy death."

From *The Notebooks of Leonardo da Vinci.*

BELOW: *One of Leonardo's drawings showing the muscles of the arm and shoulder. Such diagrams could not have been made without careful dissection of the human body.*

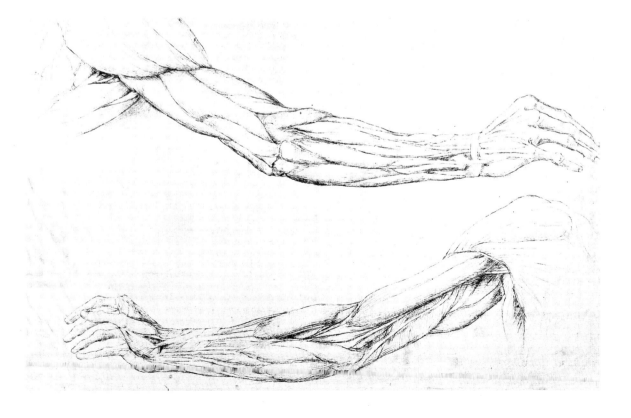

THE NOTEBOOKS

The king and Leonardo fell into conversation. Francis asked his First Painter, Architect, and Mechanic what work he had been doing. Leonardo looked a bit sheepish and confessed that he had not made much progress with his plans for the king's palace at Romorantin. He had been carried away with other matters.

When the king asked what these matters were, Leonardo explained that he had been trying to tidy up his notebooks and get them into some sort of order. He wanted them to be published one day.

Francis was fascinated. He had heard a great deal about Leonardo's famous notebooks but had never examined them carefully. Leonardo picked up a few sheets of paper from the table and passed them to the king. He apologized for the sketchy nature of his jottings and scribbles.

DA VINCI'S FLYING MACHINE

Leonardo's notebooks were full of diagrams, including several designs for flying machines. This one is like a helicopter. The screw it uses works on the same principle as a modern propeller. Leonardo's greatest difficulty was finding a way to power his machines—this one uses a metal spring.

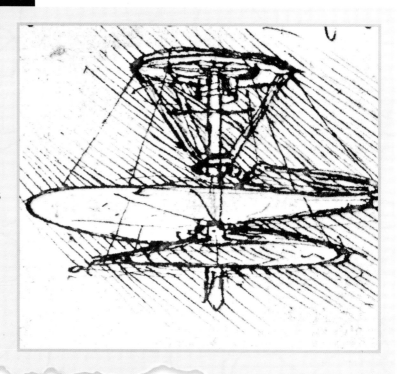

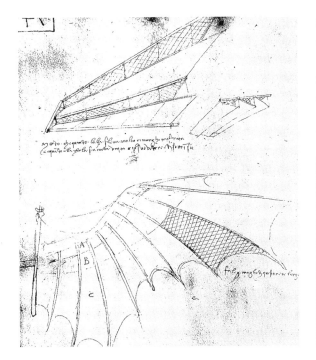

LEFT: *An alternative method of flying—Leonardo's sketch of the wings of a flying machine.*

BELOW: *In 1999 the Science Museum in London exhibited modern constructions of Leonardo's designs. This model was created using sketches from Leonardo's notebooks, including the one on the left.*

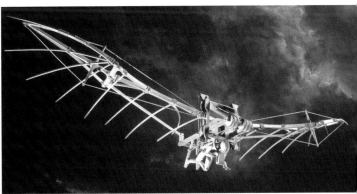

The king was not listening. He stood in silent amazement, gazing at page after page of extraordinary, brilliantly drawn machines.

What were they for, he wondered. He had no idea. Nor could he make out the writing around them. One thing he was certain of, however. They were the work of a man of an incredible and original talent.

The Greatest Genius

The year was 1517. Eight months earlier King Francis I, a keen patron of the arts, had invited Leonardo to France and housed him in a castle of his own. This was a great honor for the 65-year-old Leonardo. It was an even greater honor for the king. He knew, as did everyone else, that Leonardo was probably the greatest artistic and scientific genius the world had ever seen.

BELOW: *A contemporary illustration of King Francis I with his court. The picture is arranged to suggest the king's authority, power, and importance.*

An Exceptional Young Man

NO ONE IS sure where Leonardo was born. His surname means "from Vinci," and tradition says that his birthplace was the small Italian town of Vinci, near Florence.

The confusion arises because, at the time of Leonardo's birth (April 15, 1452), his parents were not married. His father, Ser Piero, was an official of the town of Vinci. His mother was a country girl named Caterina who later married a local man named Accattabriga. Leonardo probably lived with her for at least the first year of his life.

Piero, Leonardo's father, married Albiera di Giovanni Amadori shortly after Leonardo's birth. Albiera had no children, and by 1457 the 5-year-old Leonardo had come to live with them. We don't know about his life before this.

Not until 1476 did Piero have a legitimate son by another marriage. Leonardo, therefore, was raised as an only child.

BELOW: *A map of Italy and France during the 15ᵗʰ century, showing the places where Leonardo lived and worked.*

LEFT: *There are few pictures of Leonardo. This self-portrait shows him in middle age.*

IN THEIR OWN WORDS

THE ARTIST GIORGIO VASARI (1511–1574) SAID ART HAD REACHED A PEAK DURING ROMAN AND GREEK TIMES, THEN HAD FALLEN AWAY DURING THE MIDDLE AGES. HE BELIEVED THAT GREAT ART HAD BEEN REBORN IN RENAISSANCE ITALY:

"Once... [our artists] have seen how art reached the summit of perfection after such humble beginnings, and how it had fallen into complete ruin... they will now be able to recognize more easily the progress of art's rebirth and the state of perfection to which it has again ascended in our own times."

Renaissance Italy

Leonardo was fortunate to have been born where and when he was. Florence, the nearest large city to Vinci, was one of the richest in the world. It was a center of banking and trade. Its business families loved to display their wealth by generous spending on the arts, particularly painting and sculpture.

At this time Italy was not a single country. It was divided into separate states, such as Florence, Milan, Venice, Naples, and the Papal States (the region around Rome, ruled by the Pope). In a movement known as the Renaissance (see page 14), all forms of culture and learning were blossoming as never before throughout Italy.

AT HOME IN VINCI

Leonardo lived with his father and stepmother, Piero and Albiera, until his late teens. Their large house in Vinci belonged to Leonardo's paternal grandfather, Antonio, who also lived there with his wife, Lucia.

There are many stories about Leonardo's childhood, but few actual facts. He was fortunate to be raised in a wealthy and stimulating household. There were plenty of books to read and interesting visitors were always dropping by. As the only child in the house, he was probably a little spoiled by his parents and grandparents.

Little Latin

Leonardo was an attractive, talented child. He had a fine singing voice and showed many skills from a very young age. His education in basic reading, writing, and arithmetic was typical of the time. His stepmother and grandmother probably did most of the teaching, with tutors to help with math and Latin.

Latin was the language of learning and religion. In Renaissance Italy no one was thought well educated unless they knew Latin (and some Ancient Greek). Leonardo's Latin teacher was not very successful and his pupil never mastered classical (Latin and Greek) literature. This was probably a blessing in disguise. Leonardo's mind, uncluttered by ancient teachings, was free to go off along paths of its own.

Florence

Around 1466, Leonardo and his parents moved to Florence where his father began looking for a suitable trade or profession for his son. We are told that he showed some of Leonardo's drawings to Andrea di Cione, one of the city's finest artists. Immediately, Andrea asked to take on Leonardo as an apprentice.

IN THEIR OWN WORDS

GIORGIO VASARI SAID THE YOUNG LEONARDO COULD DO ALMOST ANYTHING:

"Truly wondrous and divine was Leonardo... and he would have made great progress in the early studies of literature if he had not been so unpredictable and unstable. For he set about learning many things and, once begun, he would then abandon them. Thus, in the few months he applied himself to arithmetic, Leonardo made such progress that he raised continuous doubts and difficulties for the master who taught him."

BELOW: *Florence, a city of timeless beauty. As in Leonardo's day, it clusters around the magnificent domed cathedral.*

THE APPRENTICE

Leonardo's master, Andrea di Cione, is better known as Verrocchio (meaning "True Eye"). Florentines prized their artists very highly, and Verrocchio's studio was about the most stimulating place in which the talented young Leonardo could have found himself.

It was alive with clever, capable people. There were Verrocchio himself, his wealthy patrons, and bright apprentices such as Botticelli and Perugino. Verrocchio was not just a painter. His studio was also a workshop. Helped by apprentices and assistants, he designed and made musical instruments, statues in stone and bronze, cannons, helmets, and many other useful and ornamental objects.

RIGHT: *Verrocchio's painting of the Madonna (Mary) and Child (Jesus). Although best known as Leonardo's teacher, Verrocchio was an important sculptor and goldsmith of the early Renaissance.*

Under Verrocchio's expert guidance, Leonardo quickly developed into a brilliant painter. Legend has it that Verrocchio was so struck by his pupil's work that he swore never to paint again. (Students of Verrocchio's work say this is untrue.)

Leonardo came to understand the subtle art of painting. He realized that before he could paint well, he had to understand why his subject looked the way it did. For him, that meant knowing how and why something worked. This led him to the study of anatomy in the next-door workshop of Antonio Pollaiuolo.

Most stories about Leonardo from this time tell the same thing. He was tall, strong, agile, and very attractive. His appeal was not just physical. Men and women, young and old, found his serenity, grace, and charm irresistible. He was aware of this, too. According to the Renaissance writer Giorgio Vasari, Leonardo liked to wander the streets in very short, brightly colored gowns. From time to time he bought a caged bird and set it free. Vasari believed that this act reflected his own free spirit and love of all life.

IN THEIR OWN WORDS

IN THE HILLS NEAR FLORENCE, LEONARDO DISCOVERED A HUGE CAVE. LOOKING IN, HE FELT FEAR AND DESIRE. THIS WAS ALSO HOW HE FELT ABOUT EXAMINING DEAD BODIES TO LEARN ABOUT HUMAN ANATOMY:

"I came to the mouth of a huge cavern, before which for a time I remained stupefied... and after remaining there for a time suddenly there were awakened within me two emotions—fear and desire—fear of the dark, threatening cavern, desire to see whether there might be any marvelous thing therein."

RIGHT: *A painting by Antonio Pollaiuolo, who taught Leonardo about anatomy. Pollaiuolo was also an accomplished painter.*

The Many-Sided Man

THE ITALIAN RENAISSANCE was at its height during Leonardo's lifetime. The word "Renaissance" means "rebirth." This refers to a growing interest in Ancient Greece and Rome that began in 14th-century Italy. From these pre-Christian civilizations came long-forgotten ideas about art, drama, science, and religion.

However, the Renaissance was more than just a fresh look at the past. Medieval Europe was deeply conservative. By and large, it accepted things as they were and fixed its attention on heaven. In contrast, Renaissance men and women paid more attention to life on Earth, to change, and to human beings and their delights.

BELOW: *The cycle of the seasons: a 13th century calendar showing farm work done in each month of the year. The wealthy citizens of Renaissance Italy were freed from such routine day-to-day activities.*

PERSPECTIVE

Renaissance artists learned how to create an impression of depth on a flat picture. We call this "perspective." The architect Filippo Brunelleschi discovered the mathematical laws of perspective in the early 15th century. Artists such as Piero della Francesca (1420–1492) and Perugino (c. 1450–1523) incorporated Brunelleschi's ideas into painting. These included the idea of a "vanishing point" in a picture, as shown in this diagram.

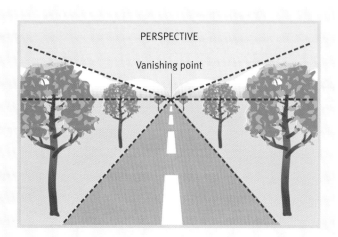

PERSPECTIVE

Vanishing point

The Spirit of Inquiry

A key feature of the Renaissance was its spirit of inquiry. Why do objects farther away look smaller? Does the Sun really go around the Earth? Why do objects fall downward? Out of such questioning, modern science and technology were born.

BELOW: *Perspective in action: a landscape by Domenico Bigordi, in which he has created a sense of distance by making distant objects smaller than nearer ones.*

A True Scientist

We live in a very specialized world. People train and work most of their lives in a single field. It is unusual, for example, for painters to make a name for themselves as poets or engineers. This was not at all the case in Leonardo's time. The ideal Renaissance Italian was "l'uomo universale," the "many-sided man." Such a person might be a number of things—soldier, artist, poet, ruler—all at once.

No one came closer to this ideal of the many-sided man than Leonardo da Vinci. His training under Verrocchio prepared him to become a painter, sculptor, designer, engineer, anatomist, writer, inventor. He searched beneath the surface, wanting to know why things looked as they did and how they worked. In short, fired by a ceaseless spirit of inquiry, he grew into a true scientist.

16

ABOVE: *A sketch of the valley of the Arno River, Leonardo's earliest known work. He was already creating his own distinctive style of drawing, later known as* chiaroscuro *(light and shade). It gave his drawing a special depth and mystery.*

MEMBER OF THE GUILD

In 1472, Leonardo was accepted as a member of the Painters' Guild of Florence. The guild was a union of the city's most skilled painters. Its purpose was to look after its members and maintain high standards of work. Membership was a great honor for the young Leonardo and a sure sign that his talent had already been recognized.

Art and Science

Leonardo's earliest known work is a drawing of the Arno Valley. Dated August 5, 1473, it shows Leonardo's mastery of the basic techniques of his profession, such as perspective and the use of light and shade.

The drawing also shows Leonardo's special blend of imagination and observation. He sees the valley as a beautiful picture, but he also tells us that he understands what he sees. He knows how the castle is built and how the fields in the background are provided with water. In his mind, imagination and observation—art and science—were not opposites. They were both tools for appreciating the world.

Art and Religion

In 1476, Leonardo and Verrocchio worked together on a painting of the baptism of Christ. This was not unusual. Masters often allowed their pupils to do the less important parts of a picture. Leonardo did the landscape and the angel at the front.

Many Renaissance pictures, such as the *Baptism of Christ*, were of religious subjects. In the 15th and 16th centuries, people didn't question religious ideas, and religion had more influence on individuals than it does today. Only the Roman Catholic Church, which was enormously rich, and a few individuals could afford works from top artists like Verrocchio. And churchmen, of course, wanted religious art.

IN THEIR OWN WORDS

LOOKING AT INDIVIDUALS, WE CAN OFTEN TELL FROM THEIR EXPRESSION AND "BODY LANGUAGE" HOW THEY FEEL. LEONARDO WANTED TO CAPTURE THIS ABILITY IN HIS PICTURES:

"A good painter has two chief objects to paint; man and the intention of his soul; the former is easy, the latter hard, because he has to represent it by the attitudes and movements of the limbs."

FROM *THE NOTEBOOKS OF LEONARDO DA VINCI*.

LEFT: *The* Baptism of Christ, *a combined effort by the master (Verrocchio) and his star pupil (Leonardo). It is interesting to compare the landscape in the background with that in the drawing on page 16, both of which are examples of Leonardo's early work.*

LORENZO THE MAGNIFICENT

Although a qualified artist by 1472, Leonardo remained in Verrocchio's workshop for another four years. Then, from 1476 to 1482, he worked independently in Florence, perhaps running his own workshop for a while.

Florence was ruled by Lorenzo, the head of the famous Medici family. Lorenzo, commonly known as "the Magnificent," was a statesman and poet. He was also a generous and wise patron of the arts. More than any other individual, he made his city the artistic capital of Europe.

BELOW: *Lorenzo de Medici, himself a poet of some ability, gave Leonardo accommodation in his palace.*

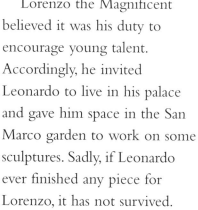

Lorenzo the Magnificent believed it was his duty to encourage young talent. Accordingly, he invited Leonardo to live in his palace and gave him space in the San Marco garden to work on some sculptures. Sadly, if Leonardo ever finished any piece for Lorenzo, it has not survived.

The Great Puzzle

This brings us to one of the most puzzling aspects of Leonardo. Why did he finish so few projects that he started? Many reasons have been suggested. One is that he was a perfectionist—he would abandon a piece of art rather than produce something less than perfect.

Another possibility is that art was not Leonardo's top priority.

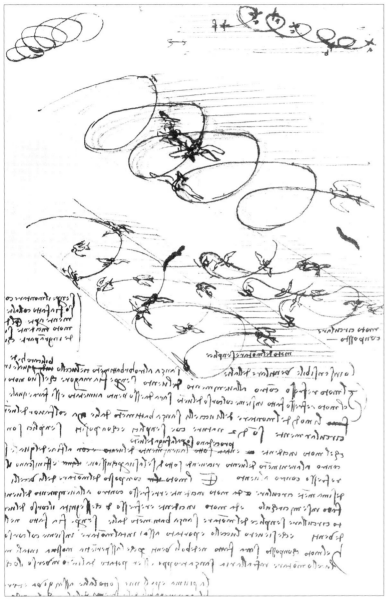

LEFT: *A page from Leonardo's notebooks in which he compares the movement of flying with that of swimming. His observations led him to write elsewhere of "the possibility that there is in man to sustain himself amid the air by the flapping of wings."*

IN THEIR OWN WORDS

VASARI EXPLAINED WHY HE THOUGHT LEONARDO LEFT SO MANY WORKS UNFINISHED:

"...he began many projects but never finished any of them, feeling that his hand could not reach artistic perfection in the works he conceived [thought of], since he envisioned [dreamed up] such subtle, marvelous, and difficult problems that his hands, while extremely skillful, were incapable of ever realizing them."

He accepted commissions for paintings and sculptures because they earned him good money. But, as he grew older, he became more interested in understanding what he painted and sculpted. To help this process, he always carried a notebook in which he jotted down ideas and opinions. As a result, Leonardo the artist left only twenty-seven brilliant paintings, but da Vinci the scientist left thousands of pages of brilliant notes.

EXPERIENCE

Although we have called Leonardo a scientist, it is not a title he would have understood. The word "scientist" was not used before 1840. Leonardo did, however, use the word "science." To him it meant knowledge proved true by experience. He contrasted it with "speculation," by which he meant guesswork not proved by experience.

It is Leonardo's emphasis on experience that makes him a scientist in our eyes. Experience, he said, is never wrong because it is based on our senses: sight, hearing, touch, taste, and smell. His notebooks are bursting with what his senses taught him.

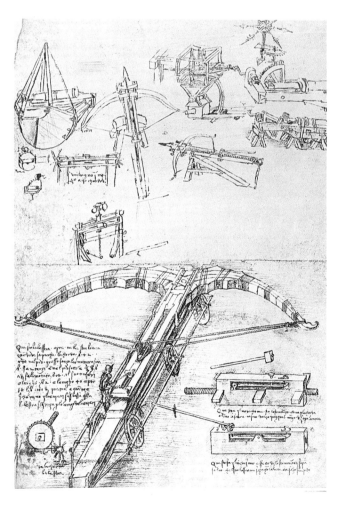

War Machines

The range of Leonardo's notebooks is vast. He wrote down just about everything that came into his mind, from philosophy to stories and jokes. His sketches, diagrams, and illustrations are, if anything, even more remarkable. In many fields, especially anatomy and engineering, he was centuries ahead of his time.

Leonardo was a man of peace. We do not hear of him becoming a soldier or even getting into a fight. Wherever he went, people said, he spread an atmosphere of harmony and calm. Nevertheless, as a young man he showed great interest in the tools of war.

LEFT: *Deadly doodles: Leonardo's design for a giant crossbow mounted on wheels. The machine was never made.*

Although we cannot be sure of the dates, it is generally agreed that while Leonardo was in Florence he was dreaming up all kinds of military machines. They included new catapults and cannon. One of the most astonishing ideas was for a "covered car, safe and unassailable" for attacking the enemy. This machine was not built for another 430-odd years. It was then named the tank.

LEONARDO'S "TANK"

Leonardo's tank could be powered either by horses or by people turning crank handles. If you look carefully at the design in the picture, you will find that the crank turns the front and back wheels in different directions! Leonardo may have done this deliberately, either because he was anti-war, or to stop someone from stealing his idea.

ABOVE: *Horsemen gathering for battle. In fact, by the later 15th century, mounted knights in armor had little importance in battle because they were too vulnerable to gunfire and the missiles of the infantry.*

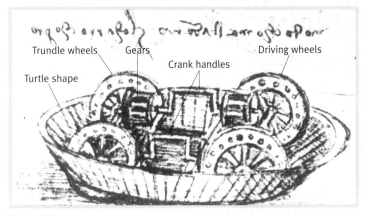

Trundle wheels   Gears   Driving wheels

Crank handles

Turtle shape

"Engineer of the Duke"

IN 1481, LEONARDO was commissioned to do two expensive and important paintings, one for the monastery of St. Donato and another for the chapel of St. Bernard, both in Florence. He finished neither work. Instead, in 1482 he left the city and traveled north to join the lavish household of the Duke of Milan. The duke wanted Leonardo to make a gigantic bronze statue, over 16 feet (5 m) high, of his father on horseback.

Like Florence, Milan was a rich city of merchants, manufacturers, and bankers. It was ruled by the Sforzas, one of the more extraordinary Renaissance families. Francesco Sforza, from a peasant family, had fought and tricked his way to become Duke of Milan in 1450. Just before Leonardo's arrival in the city, after more trickery, the dukedom had passed to one of Francesco's sons, Ludovico.

LEFT: *Francesco Sforza (1401–1466), the mercenary soldier who became Duke of Milan in 1450. Leonardo's gigantic statue of the duke was never completed.*

IN THEIR OWN WORDS

LEONARDO ASSURED DUKE LUDOVICO IN A LETTER THAT HE COULD MAKE THE STATUE THE DUKE DESIRED:

"I can carry out sculpture in marble, bronze, or clay, and also I can do, in painting whatever can be done, as well as any other.... Moreover, the bronze horse may be taken in hand [begun], which shall endue with [cover with] immortal glory and eternal honor the happy memory of the Prince your father...."

ALTHOUGH LEONARDO WORKED ON THE STATUE, ON AND OFF, FOR TWELVE YEARS, HE NEVER FINISHED IT.

The Glittering Court

The swarthy Ludovico Sforza—nicknamed "il Moro" (the Moor)—was eager for his family to be respectable. The best way, he decided, was to make his court the glittering heart of the Renaissance. Attracted by the duke's generous funding, distinguished artists, philosophers, and writers flocked to Milan.

Leonardo's arrival as "painter and engineer of the duke" was a great coup for Ludovico. He could now boast that he employed the greatest genius of his generation. For his part, Leonardo appreciated the chance to use his practical as well as his artistic skills.

At the age of 30, Leonardo was at the height of his powers. His many-sided talents were recognized throughout Italy, although he was also known for rarely finishing a piece of work. He lived in some luxury, spending freely on clothes and horses (which he adored) and always accompanied by beautiful young people.

ABOVE: *Art gives eternal life—a detail of the fresco called* **Journey of the Magi** *(the Bible's three Wise Men) to* **Bethlehem,** *in which travelers are given the faces of important 15th century Italians. Galeazzo Maria Sforza, Duke of Milan (1466–1476), is on the brown horse on the extreme left, and Sigismondo Pandolfo Malatesta (1417–1468), Lord of Rimini, is beside him on a white horse.*

ABOVE: *Leonardo's painting titled* The Last Supper. *Although ruined by the artist's use of experimental paint, which did not last, the work is still clearly a great masterpiece.*

MASTER OF CEREMONIES

Leonardo remained in Milan for seventeen years. He was well treated and—when Ludovico could find his salary—well paid. Because of his luxurious lifestyle, however, he was usually short of money. In 1498, when Ludovico hadn't the money to pay Leonardo (because the duke had spent all his money on war), he gave his artist-scientist a vineyard instead!

Ludovico, like most Renaissance princes, delighted in ceremonies. Leonardo spent hours organizing these displays. He coordinated the colors, designed the costumes, and built carts and platforms and arches. Sometimes he acted as master of ceremonies for the show itself.

Master of Arts

Leonardo's biggest project was the equestrian statue of Duke Francesco (see page 22). He eventually produced a full-size clay model of the figure but never made the statue itself, because the bronze was taken to make cannons. These weapons were needed to fight the French, who invaded Italy in 1495 and 1499 (see page 32). Later, French soldiers used the clay model for target practice.

While in Milan, Leonardo completed only six works of art. The most famous, and one of the finest pieces of art ever produced, was a wall painting of the Last Supper in the Church of Santa Maria della Grazie. Each figure was a superb mental and physical study of an individual man. Sadly, the picture fell victim to Leonardo's work habits and love of new ideas. As he painted when the mood took him, he could not use the fresco technique (see below). Instead, he painted on dry plaster with his own experimental mixture of oil and varnish. The experiment did not work, and within twenty years the paint was starting to peel and fade away. What we see today, although a brilliant restoration, is only a shadow of Leonardo's original creation.

BELOW: *A scene on the wall of the Ducale Palace, Mantua, Italy, done in fresco in the 15th century by Andrea Mantegna (1431–1506). It depicts the Marchese Ludovico Gonzaga III (second from left) and his family.*

FRESCO

Fresco painting was known to the Ancient Greeks and revived during the Renaissance. It involves covering the piece of wall to be painted with a special plaster that includes sand and marble dust. While the plaster is still wet, it is painted quickly with watercolors. The paint soaks into the plaster and becomes part of the wall. Fresco painting is very difficult because it has to be done quickly and mistakes cannot be painted over. On the other hand, it lasts for hundreds of years.

THE ARCHITECT

Leonardo was not just concerned with parades and painting. He had more practical tasks. He was consulted on the water supply to Milan Castle and how best to fortify the city. More challenging still, following a terrible outbreak of bubonic plague in 1484–1485, he devised a plan for rebuilding Milan in such a way as to make future outbreaks of the plague unlikely. Some of his ideas were more 21st than 15th century.

The new city of 300,000 inhabitants would be based around the clear waters of the Ticino River. It would be divided into ten equal districts linked by road and canal. Remarkably, Leonardo proposed a two-tier street plan: carts and other vehicles on the lower level and pedestrians on the upper. The city was never built.

LEONARDO'S WATERWHEEL

Water fascinated Leonardo, and his notebooks contain numerous plans and designs that involve water. This sketch of a waterwheel, cog wheels, and two Archimedes' screws may have been for a device to fill a raised water tank.

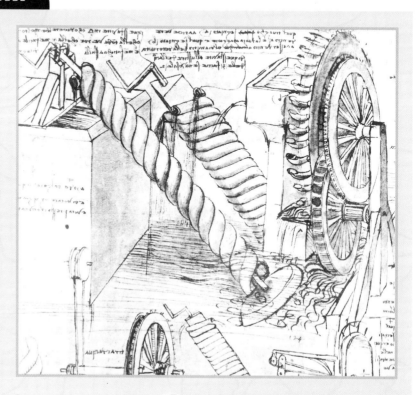

In 1487–1488, Leonardo was making a model for a new dome for Milan Cathedral. Six years later, he was offering advice for making the Martesana Canal accessible to large ships. Meanwhile, away from his official work for the duke, he continued with his own private studies.

Scientific Research

We have seen how, in order to draw or paint something, Leonardo wanted to see beneath its surface (see page 16). Nothing he drew was more complicated than the human body. In Florence, he had studied anatomy. In Milan he went even further—he began dissecting human corpses to see what muscles and bones were there.

By now, Leonardo's studies were not simply an aspect of his art. He did not examine the heart, brain, and lungs, for example, in order to draw better. He wanted to know precisely how these organs worked and what their purpose was. In other words, he was engaged in scientific research.

BELOW-LEFT: *Always the artist: Leonardo's artistic instinct meant that even when he was drawing part of the nervous system (as here), he gave his model a distinct personality.*

BELOW: *The brain and its links with the rest of the body. Leonardo's technique of recording his observations was the beginning of modern scientific drawing.*

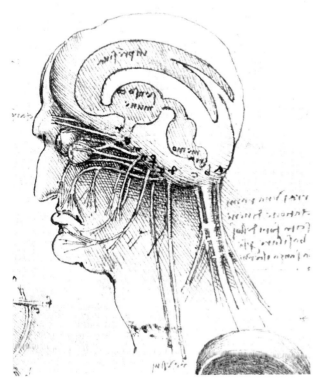

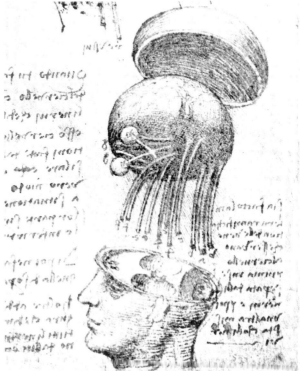

SELF-SUFFICIENCY

Because of what we read in Leonardo's notebooks, we know more about his mind than about his body, his emotions, and his everyday life. He seems to have been quite a self-sufficient man. We know, for example, that he never married and had no children. He had many friends and companions, but he seems to have directed his most intense emotions not toward people but into his remarkable studies.

BELOW-RIGHT: *An aerial view of Leonardo's horseless carriage.*

LEONARDO'S HORSELESS CARRIAGE

Leonardo sketched several land vehicles. The one shown here was driven by springs that moved the wheels through a series of cogs. The precise details of how Leonardo thought it would work are not at all clear. The driver was kept busy steering and, at the same time, winding up springs that had run down.

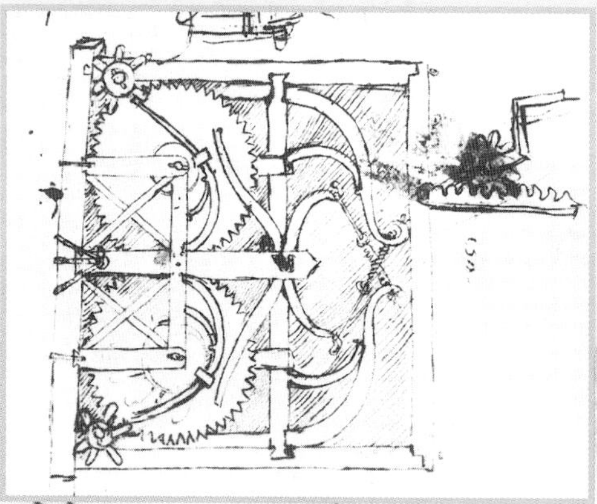

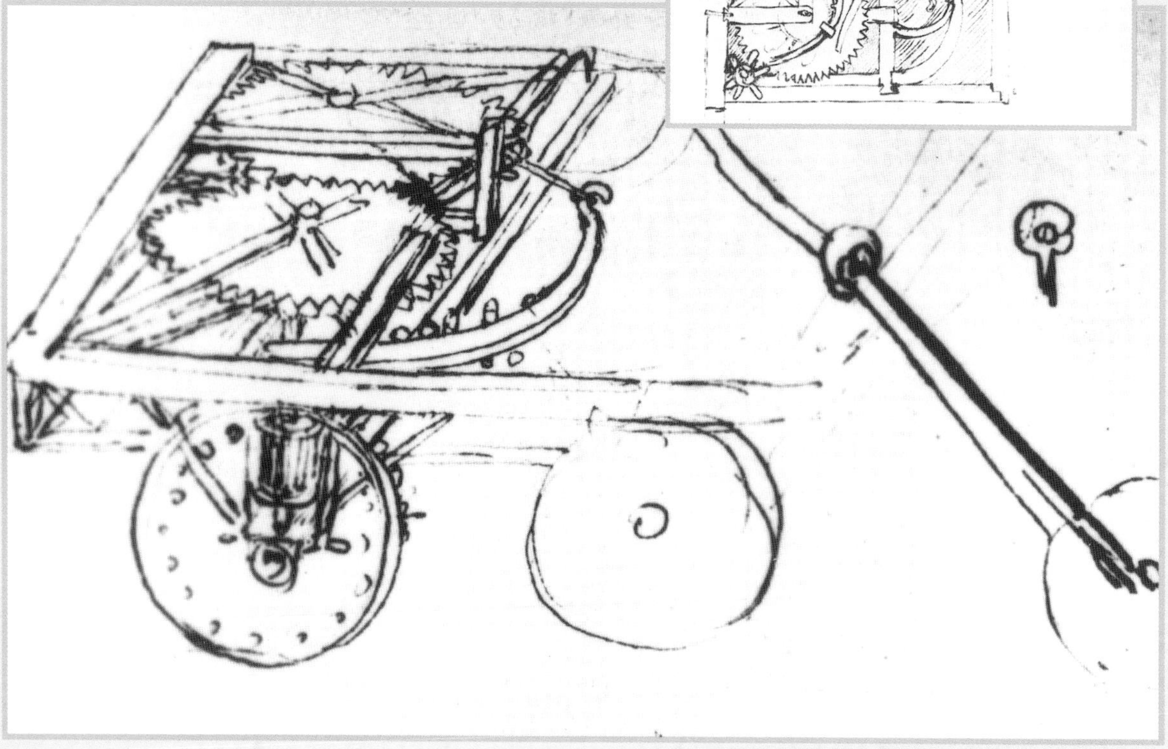

The Great Project

By the 1490s, Leonardo was taking a new attitude toward his notes. Previously he had jotted down ideas and inventions pretty much as they came into his mind. (He even carried miniature notebooks in his belt, ready for use at any moment!) Now, nearing the end of his time in Milan, he wanted his research to be more organized and systematic. This is a clear indication of his scientific way of thinking.

Leonardo was inspired by men like Leon Battista Alberti, author of a ten-volume science of architecture published in 1485. Leonardo's aim was to produce a similar kind of book on painting—a science of painting. In time he expanded the project to take in anatomy and mechanics. Eventually, he set himself the task of seeing and recording every visible thing in the world.

It is hardly surprising to find that he was still working on this project when living at Cloux twenty years later.

ABOVE: *Leon Battista Alberti (1404–1472), the Italian architect who greatly admired and copied the Roman style of building.*

THE STRUCTURE OF THE ANKLE

In the 15th century, the way the human body worked was understood only imperfectly. The normal approach was to start with a theory, then apply that theory to a body. Leonardo did things the other way around. He started with observation, then developed theories from what he had observed.

These drawings of a human calf, thigh, and hamstring show his scientific method in action. By careful observation, Leonardo has worked out precisely the combination of muscles and tendons that form the leg.

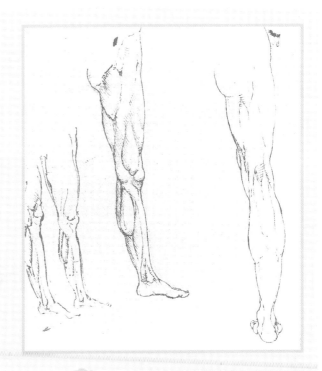

PRACTICAL DEVICES

BELOW: *Here is an example of how Leonardo's designs were based on scientific principle. On the left is a picture from his notebook. On the right is a modern construction of the parachute, based entirely on Leonardo's design. As you can see, it works perfectly.*

Leonardo's scientific projects were years, even centuries, ahead of his time. The most obvious thing we notice is that he thought up devices—a tank, flying machine, submarine, double-hulled vessel, and so forth—long before they were actually made.

This in itself was not so special. Many people come up with similarly fanciful doodles. What made Leonardo's dream machines different was that he based them on scientific

LEONARDO'S PARACHUTE

In one of his notebooks, Leonardo wrote, "If a man makes a linen tent, 12 feet across and 12 feet deep, with all its openings closed, he'll be able to jump from any height without injury."

This "linen tent" is what we call a parachute. In recent years, researchers have built full-scale versions of Leonardo's device, using canvas and wood, and found that it really does work.

principles. Unlike many modern science-fiction books and films, for example, Leonardo did not use technology that had not been discovered. His machines were practical and stood a chance of working.

Scientific Method

Leonardo's scientific method was also ahead of its time. In his day, men of learning strove to prove principles. Most of these principles (for example, God made the world in seven days, or that blood goes straight up and down the body) were derived from the Bible or classical authorities.

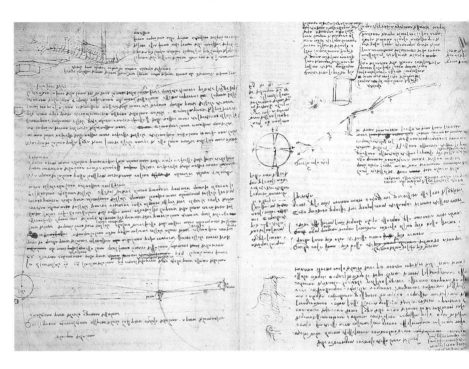

ABOVE: *Two pages from Leonardo's notebooks showing his right to left ("mirror") handwriting, without punctuation. The language is Italian, not classical Greek or Latin. Like a modern textbook, the diagrams fall within the text.*

Leonardo turned this method on its head. He observed first, then drew up principles from his observations (or "experiences"—see page 20). This style of reasoning did not become widespread until the Scientific Revolution of the 17th century. It led Leonardo to ideas that, had he made them public, would have landed him in serious trouble. For instance, he appeared to mistrust the biblical age of the Earth. According to his observations, it was much older than the Bible said. Also, contrary to what was taught in all places of learning, he appeared to believe that blood circulated around the body.

Pictures Before Words

Finally, Leonardo's notebooks show a new relationship between illustration (which he called "demonstration") and text. For years, scientific books used pictures to illustrate the text. Leonardo's words clarify the illustration. This is the basic principle of all modern scientific illustration.

Moving On

LIFE IN RENAISSANCE Italy was never settled for long. Not only were the individual states (see map on page 8) continually squabbling, but at the end of the 15th century the rich Italian peninsula had become a tempting target for outsiders. The most powerful of the region's enemies were the French.

In the summer of 1499 the French king, Louis XII, in alliance with Venice and the Pope, swept into Milan and occupied the city. Duke Ludovico had already fled. A few months later Leonardo, too, left the city. Traveling with his friend Luca Pacioli, a favorite pupil, Andrea Salai, and other companions and servants, he went first to Mantua before moving on to Venice the following March.

BELOW: *Venice in the late 15th century. The great port was one of the few Italian cities not to be ruled by a single person or family.*

Back to Florence

Leonardo was by now what we would call a "major celebrity." The Venetians welcomed him warmly and asked his advice on defending part of their territory against a possible attack from the Turks. Leonardo, obsessed as ever with water, suggested they flood it. He then left Venice and crossed Italy to Florence, arriving in April 1500.

Leonardo's father, Piero, was now in his mid-70s. He must have been delighted to see his son again. Of Leonardo's mother, Caterina, we know nothing certain. In 1504, the year of Piero's death, Leonardo recorded paying the medical bills and burial expenses of a woman named "Caterina." She was likely to have been his mother or a servant. It would be pleasing—and in keeping with his kind personality—to think that it was his mother and he had kept in touch with her all the years he had been away.

BELOW: *A 15th century painting showing travelers on horseback approaching a city. Leonardo would have traveled around Italy in a similar fashion.*

ABOVE: *Cesare Borgia, Duke of Romagna (1476–1507).*

MAP MAKER

However pleased Leonardo was to be among old friends and family again, he did not stay long in Florence. He worked as an artist and architect, before going south to Rome in 1502. His new position was "senior military architect and general engineer" to the Duke of Romagna, Cesare Borgia.

The duke, the illegitimate son of Pope Alexander VI, was one of the great villains of his time. He had used his father's armies to conquer most of central Italy (1499–1502). Leonardo's job was to survey this area, so that the duke would know how much land he had gained. Why he took it on, we do not know. He was probably fascinated by the 27-year-old Cesare's dynamic, wicked personality.

Leonardo traipsed around Cesare's lands, met the philosopher Nicolo Machiavelli, and produced a delightful selection of maps, plans, and drawings. In 1503 he was back in Florence, where he made plans to divert the Arno River and build a canal linking Florence to the sea. He also began (but never finished) several works of art.

LEONARDO'S PLAN OF IMOLA

Leonardo drew this remarkable plan of the town of Imola in 1502. Some scholars believe it is one of the first geometric town plans ever produced. Although Leonardo liked his maps to look like pieces of art, his work in this field helped lay the foundations of modern cartography.

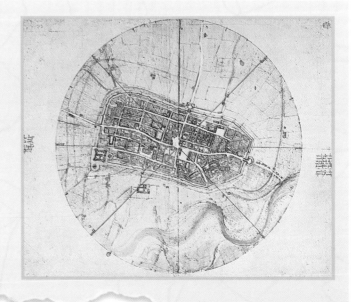

The *Mona Lisa*

Leonardo did just about complete one work, although he never parted with it and always said it was unfinished. This is the painting known as the *Mona Lisa*, perhaps the most famous picture in the world. Georgio Vasari reported that Leonardo employed musicians and clowns to keep his subject smiling as he worked on her portrait!

Meanwhile, Leonardo went on with his private studies. He was spending a good deal of time on anatomy, basing his work on extensive dissections in the St. Maria Nuova hospital.

LEFT: *Leonardo's* Mona Lisa, *also known as* "La Gioconda" *after the name of its Neapolitan subject. Now on display in the Louvre Museum in Paris, it is visited by thousands of people every year.*

ABOVE: *A sketch for the* Battle of Anghiari, *one of the many paintings that Leonardo never completed.*

BELOW: *Charles d'Amboise, the French governor of Milan, who invited Leonardo to the city in 1506.*

ART BEFORE CASH

Leonardo was never very wealthy. When his father died in 1504, his half-brothers and sisters managed to trick him out of his inheritance. What money he earned, he spent freely on maintaining his large household of friends, servants, and pupils. He could have made more, of course, particularly if he had finished his commissions.

In 1503, for example, Leonardo began a vast mural, twice the size of his *Last Supper*. It was entitled *Battle of Anghiari*. Although he did brilliant sketches for the piece and worked on it for three years, he left Florence without completing it. A different artist might have finished the mural to receive his full payment. But Leonardo put art before money—if he could not get a picture exactly right, he had to leave it, whatever the cost.

Return to Milan

Leonardo left his *Battle of Anghiari* in 1506, when the French governor of Milan, Charles d'Amboise, invited him there for a three-month stay. Both d'Amboise and King Louis XII of France wanted the prestige of employing the almost legendary Leonardo. Indeed, they treated the 54-year-old artist-scientist so well that he remained in Milan for much of the next seven years.

Maintained by a generous royal pension and given little work, Leonardo was free to do what he enjoyed most. Many talented young artists flocked to his workshop to see Leonardo's work and meet the great man. In his ample spare time, he pressed on with his researches. These were becoming more mathematical and theoretical. Pondering force and motion, he came to two extraordinary conclusions.

First, he decided that there were fixed laws that determined all movement. Later, these were worked out as the laws of mechanics. Second, he toyed with the idea that movement and existence were somehow related. Only in the 20th century was such an idea shown to be true.

IN THEIR OWN WORDS

LEONARDO'S DISCUSSION OF FRICTION WAS CLEARLY BASED ON HIS OWN OBSERVATION:

"If a ten-pound hammer drives a nail into a piece of wood with one blow, a hammer of one pound will not drive the nail altogether into the wood in ten blows. Nor will a nail that is less than a tenth part (of the first) be buried more deeply by the said hammer of a pound in a single blow... because the hardness of the wood does not diminish the proportion of its resistance."

FROM *THE NOTEBOOKS OF LEONARDO DA VINCI.*

LEFT: *A drawing to show how water might be raised to the top of a high water tower. It involves a smaller tower with a tank on it, two Archimedes' screws, and a waterwheel.*

Honored Guest

IN 1513, THE French were driven from Milan. Leonardo, now age 60, went to Rome to resume his relationship with the Medicis (see page 18). Duke Giuliano de Medici, the brother of Pope Leo X, gave Leonardo comfortable accommodations and a good income. He demanded little work of him. Leonardo had become a sort of trophy, a silver cup for display only.

Research Before Art

Like a modern medical student, Leonardo knew he could not understand how the body worked unless he looked inside it. This meant dissecting corpses. Unfortunately, the Pope had banned dissection in Rome. This left Leonardo to paint a little and wander around monuments of the Eternal City, as Rome was called. For the duke he produced a few sketches and a wonderful map of the Pontine Marshes.

BELOW: *The Eternal City: Rome in the early 16th century, when Duke Giuliano de Medici invited Leonardo to stay there.*

LEFT: *Pope Leo X (1475–1521), brother of Duke Giuliano de Medici. He was an admirer of Leonardo's work, but banned him from dissecting corpses.*

In his plentiful spare time, Leonardo experimented with balloons and mirrors. He also changed a tame lizard into a dragon by equipping it with artificial wings, a horn, and a beard. Clearly, he was far happier doing research than starting a work of art he knew he probably could never get quite right.

Pope Leo discovered this when he asked Leonardo for a painting. The artist immediately began experimenting with varnish for the finished picture. In despair, the Pope exclaimed, "Alas, this man is never going to do anything, for he starts to think about finishing the work before it is even begun!'"

To France

The other great artist of Leonardo's day was Michelangelo Buonarotti, who had publicly scoffed at Leonardo for his failure to finish so many pieces of work. The two did not get along, so in 1516, lonely and wanting to distance himself from Michelangelo, Leonardo accepted an invitation from King Francis I to move to France.

BELOW: *Michelangelo Buonarroti (1475–1564), the only other Renaissance figure whose reputation matches that of Leonardo. Unfortunately, the two men did not get along.*

BATAILLE DE MARIGNAN
GAGNÉE PAR FRANÇOIS I
14 Septembre 1515

ABOVE: *Francis I in battle. Like many warrior kings of the time, such as England's Henry VIII, Francis was also a generous patron of arts and learning.*

THE ARTIST AND THE KING

King Francis had been leading a war campaign in Italy in 1516. After defeating the armies of Leo X, he held secret negotiations with the Pope. At one of these meetings, perhaps, Francis first met Leonardo.

A bond of mutual respect and admiration immediately formed between the triumphant young king and the aged artist. Francis had a keen mind and genuinely liked the arts. He invited Leonardo to France because he felt it was only right that the greatest living genius should be allowed to pass his declining years in peace and comfort.

So it was that when the victorious French army returned home from Italy during the winter of 1516, the 65-year-old Leonardo traveled with it. He was accompanied by his favorite and most loyal pupil, Francesco Melzi. In France,

Leonardo was established as "First Painter, Architect, and Mechanic" of the realm and accommodated in the small but comfortable château of Cloux on the Loire River.

The Final Visit

The artist Benvenuto Cellini said the king often visited Cloux just to hear Leonardo talk (see Chapter 1). Indeed, so frequent were these royal visits that they may have hampered Leonardo's efforts to get his notebooks in order before his death.

Leonardo had a stroke shortly after arriving in France, and he made his will on April 23, 1519. A few days later, feeling the end was close, he asked about Roman Catholic teaching, some of which he had questioned in his researches. After a priest had explained carefully how a Christian soul could go to heaven, Leonardo confessed his sins to God. Finally, on May 2, he apologized for neglecting his painting, laid his head back on the pillows, and quietly passed away.

IN THEIR OWN WORDS

GIORGIO VASARI MET MANY PEOPLE WHO HAD KNOWN LEONARDO. HE ALSO SAW HIS PICTURES, INCLUDING *THE LAST SUPPER*, AT THEIR FRESHEST AND FINEST.

"The loss of Leonardo saddened beyond all measure everyone who had known him, for no one ever lived who had brought so much honor to painting. His splendidly handsome appearance could bring calm to every troubled soul, and his words could sway the most hardened mind to either side of a question.... His generosity was so great that he sheltered and fed all his friends, rich and poor alike.... By his every action [he] adorned and honored the meanest and humblest dwelling place; and with his birth, Florence truly received the greatest of all gifts, and at his death, the loss was incalculable."

LEFT: *A romanticized painting of Leonardo on his deathbed, with King Francis (center) by his side.*

Talent Beyond Measure

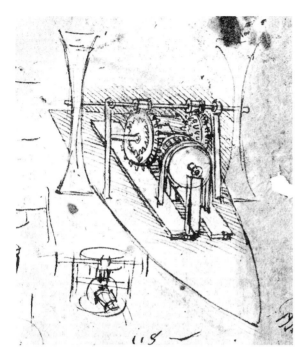

ABOVE: *Leonardo's design for a paddleboat. Such a ship was not constructed for another 300 years.*

BELOW: *Designs for flippers to be attached to the hands and feet. Again, Leonardo's idea was hundreds of years ahead of its time.*

LEONARDO LEFT NO invention that altered people's lives, nor did he make a discovery that changed how we understand the world. He had no scientific education and published no scientific paper. He worked only to satisfy his own curiosity. And yet we honor him as a great scientist. Why?

Three features make Leonardo's talent truly unique. The first is his scientific method. He used evidence presented to him by his senses, not found secondhand in ancient and honored texts. This manner of reasoning was widely adopted in the 17th century and revolutionized the way we think. Leonardo anticipated this revolution by more than a century.

Breadth and Originality

The second remarkable feature of Leonardo's work was its breadth. His twenty-seven finished paintings are all treasures. The *Mona Lisa* is regarded as an almost perfect picture. Moreover, out of his training as a painter, and his ability to observe in great detail, came ground-breaking scientific work. His discoveries, theories, and experiments were of staggering breadth. They ranged from theoretical physics and mechanics to architecture, hydrography, physiology, and biology.

The third and perhaps most eye-catching feature of Leonardo's work was its originality. Hundreds of years before such things appeared, we find in his notebooks sketches and plans for flying machines, mechanical vehicles, a submarine, a parachute, tanks, machine guns, and dozens of other astounding gadgets and devices.

Reaching to Heaven

All this amounts to a talent beyond measure. Leonardo was one of a kind, a genius we can only marvel at and respect. Add his gentle and kindly personality, and we can see why Vasari wrote of the "truly wondrous and divine" Leonardo: "Through his mind and the excellence of his intellect we may reach to heaven."

BELOW: *Leonardo's* Annunciation, *showing the archangel Gabriel visiting the Virgin Mary with the good news that she would be the mother of Jesus. Although a conventional subject at that time, Leonardo gave it a special magic all his own.*

IN THEIR OWN WORDS

MANY ARGUE THAT LEONARDO IS BEST REMEMBERED NOT FOR WHAT HE DID BUT FOR HOW HE DID IT. HIS RELIANCE UPON "EXPERIENCE" (WHAI WE CALL EVIDENCE) WAS TRULY REVOLUTIONARY:

"Many will think that they can with reason blame me, alleging that my proofs are contrary to the authority of certain men held in great reverence..., not considering that my works are the issue of simple and plain experience which is the true mistress. ... Though I have no power to quote from authors..., I shall rely on a far bigger and more worthy thing—on experience, the instructress of the [ir] masters."

FROM *THE NOTEBOOKS OF LEONARDO DA VINCI.*

Timeline

c.1266

Birth of Giotto (di Bondone), the artist who sowed the seeds of the Renaissance in Italian art. (Died 1337)

1386

Work begins on Milan Cathedral. Renaissance artist Donatello born.

1401

Francesco Sforza, the future Duke of Milan, born. Masaccio, famous perspective painter, born.

1420

Florence Cathedral finished.

1450

Francesco Sforza becomes Duke of Milan.

1452

APRIL 15: Leonardo born in or near Vinci, a village near Florence, Italy.

1453

Turks capture Constantinople; classical scholars flee Constantinople and settle in Western Europe.

1457

Leonardo living with his father and stepmother in Vinci.

1466

Leonardo and his parents move to Florence. Leonardo becomes an apprentice in the workshop of Verrocchio.

1472

Lorenzo de Medici ("the Magnificent") becomes ruler of Florence.

1473

Leonardo draws his earliest known work, *The Arno Valley*.

1475

Michelangelo born.

1476

Leonardo leaves Verrocchio's workshop and works on his own until 1482.

1481

Ludovico Sforza becomes Duke of Milan. Leonardo writes to him, offering his services.

1482

Duke Ludovico sends for Leonardo, who enters his service. Leonardo devotes time to his researches and notebooks.

1483

Birth of famous Renaissance artist Raphael.

1484–1485

Outbreak of plague in Milan.

1485

Leon Battista Alberti's book on Roman architecture published.

1487

Leonardo makes a model for a dome for Milan Cathedral. He begins his study of anatomy.

1492

Leonardo visits Rome. Leonardo designs a flying machine.

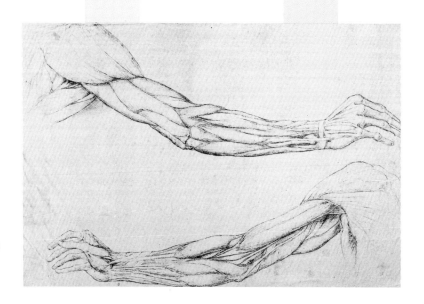

1516

Francis I meets Leonardo in Italy and invites him to France; he settles in the château of Cloux.

1517

Leonardo suffers a stroke that paralyzes his right side.

1519

MAY 2: Leonardo dies and is buried in church of Saint-Florentin, within the royal château of Amboise.

1564

Michelangelo dies.

1789

Beginning of French Revolution, in which Leonardo's grave is despoiled and eventually lost.

1493

Clay model of statue of Francesco Sforza finished.

1495

Leonardo begins his *Last Supper* mural (to 1498).

1498

Leonardo given a vineyard by Duke Ludovico. Michaelangelo completes his famous statue, *Pietà*.

1499

Louis XII of France occupies Milan. Leonardo leaves Milan for Mantua and Venice. Francesco Sforza driven from Milan.

1500

Leonardo returns to Florence.

1502

Leonardo goes to Rome to work for Cesare Borgia.

1503

Leonardo returns to Florence; begins *Battle of Anghiari* mural and *Mona Lisa*.

1504

Leonardo's father dies (and perhaps his mother, too).

1505

Leonardo studies the flight of birds.

1506

French invite Leonardo back to Milan. Rebuilding of St Peter's Cathedral, Rome, begins.

1507

Leonardo visits Florence.

1510

Leonardo explains the principles of the water turbine.

1511

Giorgio Vasari born.

1513

French driven from Milan; Leonardo goes to Rome at the request of Giuliano de Medici.

1515

Death of Louis XII. Francis I becomes king of France.

Glossary

anatomy study of the physical structure of a body.

apprentice someone working with a qualified employer to learn a craft or trade.

Archimedes screw device for moving water uphill, invented by the ancient Greek philosopher Archimedes.

architecture study of the design and construction of buildings.

biology study of all forms of life.

bronze metal made up of copper and tin.

cartography study of maps and map-making.

château French castle or country house.

commission to pay an artist to do a particular piece of work.

crank rod, such as an axle, with a bend in it so that up and down motion can be converted into circular motion. A bicycle pedal is a common example of a crank.

dissect to cut into parts in order to examine carefully.

double-hull a ship with two outer skins or layers.

equestrian of horses or horseback riding.

Florentines people of Florence.

fresco wall or ceiling painting done on fresh plaster.

geometric according to the rules of geometry.

guild organization of expert craftworkers. It aims to uphold standards of workmanship and look after its members.

hydrography study of seas and other bodies of water.

medieval of the Middle Ages.

Middle Ages period of European history, roughly 700–1450 A.D.

mural wall painting.

patron one who supports a person or an activity with money.

peninsula finger of land surrounded on three sides by water.

perfectionist one who wants everything he or she does to be perfect.

philosophy love of wisdom, ideas, and learning.

physiology science of the processes of life.

profession job that requires academic training.

psychology science of the mind.

Renaissance period of European history when the arts and learning blossomed. It started in Italy in about 1350 and continued to about 1550. One of its features was a new interest in ancient Greece and Rome.

revolution complete, swift, and often permanent change.

statesman wise and experienced ruler.

studio artist's workshop.

unassailable unable to be attacked.

vineyard where vines grow.

Further Information

BOOKS FOR YOUNGER READERS

Connolly, Sean. *The Life and Work of Leonardo da Vinci*. Chicago: Heinemann Library, 1999.

Herbert, Janis. *Leonardo da Vinci for Kids: His Life and Ideas*. Chicago: Chicago Review Press, 1998.

Kuhne, Heinz. *Leonardo da Vinci: Dreams, Schemes, and Flying Machines*. New York: Prestel USA, 2000.

Malam, John. *Leonardo da Vinci*. North Pomfret, VT: Evans Brothers, 1998.

Stanley, Diane. *Leonardo da Vinci*. New York: HarperCollins Children's Books, 2000.

Venezia, Mike. *Getting to Know the World's Greatest Artists: Leonardo da Vinci*. Danbury, CT: Children's Press, 1994.

BOOKS FOR OLDER READERS

Barcilon, Pinin Brambilla. *Leonardo: The Last Supper*. Chicago: University of Chicago Press, 2001.

da Vinci, Leonardo. *The Notebooks of Leonardo da Vinci*. Mineola, NY: Oxford University Press, 1988.

Gelb, Michael J. *The How to Think Like Leonardo da Vinci Workbook and Notebook: Your Personal Companion to How to Think Like Leonardo da Vinci*. New York: Bantam Books, 1999.

Nuland, Sherwin B. *Leonardo da Vinci*. New York: Viking Press, 2000.

WEBSITES

http://www.museoscienza.org/english/leonardo/leonardo.html
An online exhibit from The National Museum of Science and Technology of Milan, which details Leonardo da Vinci's life through biological information and photos.

http://www.leonet.it/comuni/vincimus/invinmus.html
The official website of the Leonardo da Vinci Museum in Vinci. This site gives a tour of the different da Vinci artwork that can be found throughout the museum.

http://www.carmensandiego.com/products/time/davincic11/ebmain_c11.html
This web site is devoted to artists emerging through the Renaissance period.

http://www.mos.org/sln/Leonardo/
Readers can learn about Leonardo da Vinci's inventions, paintings, and mirror-image writings.

Index